It was August and the children were on holiday with Gran.

"Hello, my name is Dawn," said the woman at the door. "Do come in."

"Why don't you children go and play with Floppy?" said Gran.

Kipper threw a ball for Floppy. Suddenly, a puppy ran up and caught it.

A girl ran up and took the ball.
"You are a naughty puppy!" said the girl.

"My name is Paula," she said. "I'm Dawn's daughter. And this is Dorā."

"Oh no!" said Paula. "Where is she going now?"

The puppy was digging up the lawn. Floppy put his paw on the puppy to stop her.

"Would you like to see the tree house?" asked Paula.

"Wow!" said Chip. "Can we go up?"
"Yes," said Paula. "I'll tell Mum where
you are."

Floppy squeezed under the gate. They all followed.

They saw Floppy scratching at the
cellar door.

"See," said Kipper. "It is haunted!"
"Well," said Gran. "Let's see."

Gran opened the door to the cellar, and the noise got louder. Floppy ran in.

There was a girl playing the trumpet, and a boy was singing. Dora was there, too.

The players stopped when they saw
Floppy. He barked at Dora.

"It's Paula!" said Biff.
"So the house isn't haunted," said Gran.

"It's for my mum's birthday," said Paula. "The four of us have just started playing."

"Would you like to hear us play?" asked Paula. "We're not very good yet!"

Floppy started howling like a wolf.
"He wants to join the band!" said Biff.